This book should be returned to any branch of the
Lancashire County Library on or before the date shown

ı ı\ı ч

ı 6 . 7 . ı S

2 3 AUG 2019

NTH

2 8 NOV 2018

1 3 FEB 2020

6ı0Z ʎⱯW Ɫ Z

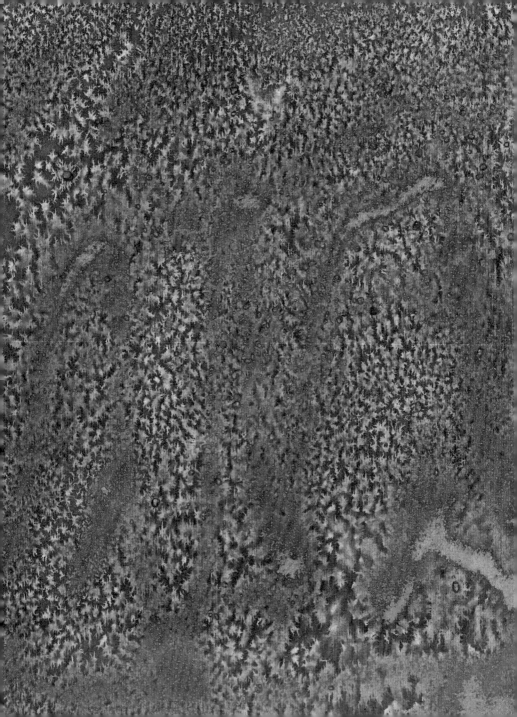

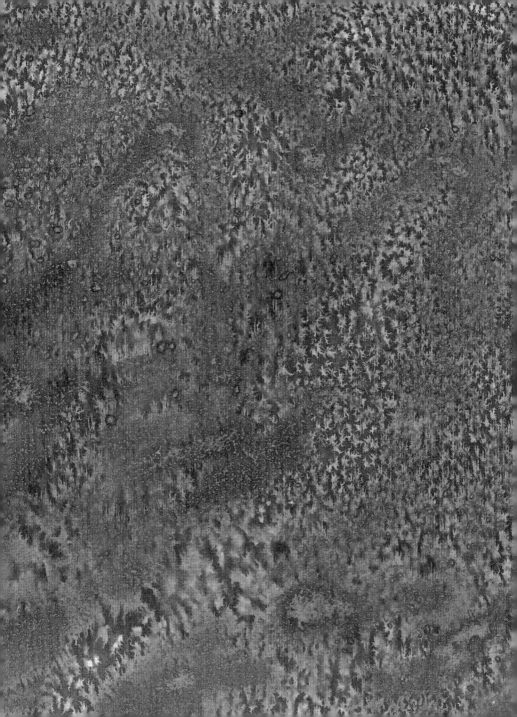

For Osky Bosky Boy (Oscar)

Text and Illustrations copyright M.P. Robertson 2000, 2014

The right of M.P. Robertson to be identified as the author and illustrator of this Work has been asserted by him in accordance with the Copyright, Designs and Patent Act, 1988.

First published in Great Britain in 2000.

This early reader edition first published in Great Britain and in the USA in 2014 by Frances Lincoln Children's Books, 74-77 White Lion Street, London N1 9PF

www.franceslincoln.com

A CIP catalogue record for this book is available from the British Library.

978-1-84780-551-5

Printed in China

1 3 5 7 9 8 6 4 2

The
EGG

M.P. Robertson

F
FRANCES LINCOLN
CHILDREN'S BOOKS

George knew something was not right when he found something curious under his mother's best chicken.

He moved the egg to his warm bedroom.

For three days and three nights he read stories to the egg.

On the third night, the egg started to rumble.

Something was hatching, and it definitely wasn't
a chicken . . .

When the dragon saw George, it gave a cheep
of delight.
George didn't speak Dragon, but he knew exactly
what the dragon had said . . .

"Mummy."
George had never been a mother before, but he
knew that he must do his duty to teach the dragon
dragony ways.

 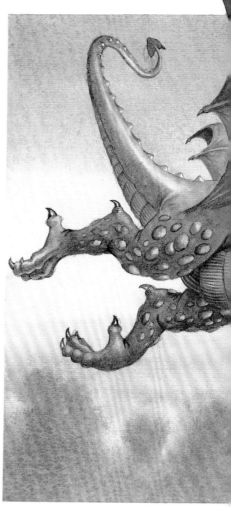

The first lesson he taught was The Fine Art of Flying.

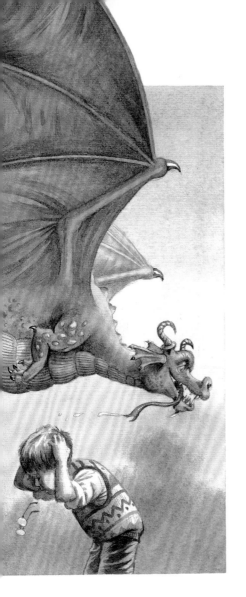

The second lesson was Fire and How to Breathe It.

The third lesson was How to Distress a Damsel.

And the final lesson was How to Fight a Knight.

Every evening, George read the dragon a bedtime
story, as good mothers do.
When he read from a book of dragon tales, the
dragon looked sadly at the pictures.

A hot tear rolled down his scaly cheek.
The dragon was lonely. He was missing
other dragons.

The next morning, the dragon had gone. George
was very sad. He thought he would never see his
dragon again.

But seven nights later, he woke up to the sound of
beating wings. He pulled back the curtains.
There was the dragon, sitting in a tree. George
opened the window and clambered onto his back.

They soared into the night, chasing the moon around
the world, over oceans and mountains and cities.

Faster and faster they went, until they came to a
place that was neither North nor South, East nor West.

They swooped down through the clouds, into a cave like a dragon's jaws. This was the place where dragons lived.

The dragon gave a roar of delight. He was home at last.

Finally, it was time for George to leave.
Up, up they flew, chasing sleep through
the night, until they could see his home below.

George hugged his dragon tight, and the dragon gave a roar. George didn't speak Dragon, but he knew exactly what the dragon had said . . . "Thank you."

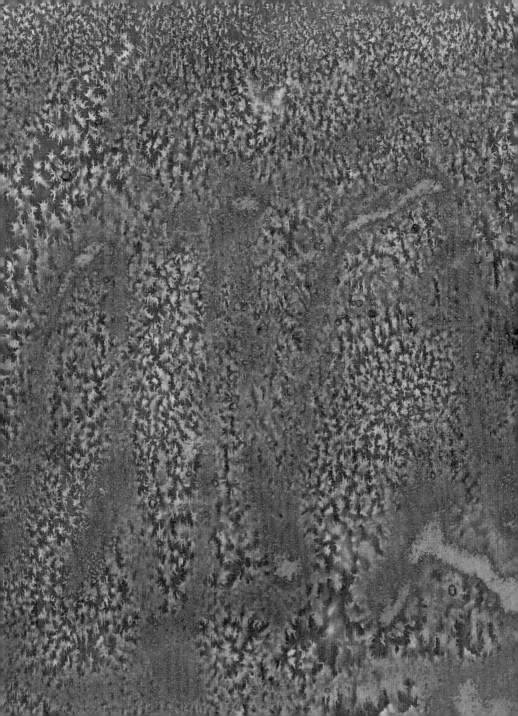